ERMINE'S NEW HOME

by Stephanie Smith

Illustrated by Robert Hynes

Little® Soundprints

To my family, who supported me when it was time for me to leave the den—S.S.

To my family—R.H.

Book design: Marcin D. Pilchowski
Editor: Laura Gates Galvin
Editorial assistance: Chelsea Shriver

First Edition 2002
10 9 8 7 6 5 4 3 2
Printed in China

Acknowledgments:
        Our very special thanks to Dr. Don E. Wilson of the Department of Systematic Biology at the Smithsonian Institution's National Museum of Natural History for his curatorial review, and our very special thanks to Robert Hynes for his amazing work under pressure.
        Soundprints would also like to thank Ellen Nanney and Robyn Bissette at the Smithsonian Institution's Office of Product Development and Licensing for their help in the creation of this book.

Library of Congress Cataloging-in-Publication Data

Smith, Stephanie, 1976-
Ermine's new home / by Stephanie Smith ; illustrated by Robert Hynes.
                p. cm.
Summary: An ermine leaves his family's den to find a home of his own.
ISBN 1-931465-18-5 (hardcover) — ISBN 1-931465-17-7 (pbk.)
1. Ermine—Juvenile fiction. [1. Ermine—Fiction.] I. Hynes, Robert, ill. II. Title.

PZ10.3.S6548 Er 2002
[Fic]—dc21

2001049687

Table of Contents

Chapter 1: Ermine's Family   5

Chapter 2: The Cold Winter   15

Chapter 3: Danger!   27

Chapter 4: Home at Last   35

Glossary   44

Wilderness Facts About the Ermine   45

A note to the reader:
Throughout this story you will see words in **bold letters**.
There is more information about these words in the
glossary. The glossary is in the back of the book.

Chapter 1

Ermine's Family

It is a warm summer day. An **ermine** wakes up in his **den**. His den is under the ground. Ermine is only a few months old. Ermine has three brothers and two sisters. They play together.

The ermine family lives on the **tundra**. The tundra is a rocky place. There are many predators on the tundra. Predators like to eat smaller animals. When Ermine is older, he will learn to defend himself.

For now, the ermine babies must stay inside. Their mother is out hunting. She will catch mice for them to eat. It is Ermine's favorite food!

In a few weeks, the
ermine babies are old
enough to leave the
den. Ermine spends the
summer learning to
hunt. He watches his
mother. She catches
mice and **shrews**.

Now it is October. The young ermines are ready to live by themselves. Ermine leaves the den one day. He needs to find his new home. His brothers and sisters will leave, too.

Chapter 2

The Cold Winter

Ermine walks across the tundra. He walks through the forest. He is looking for a place with plenty of food. He also needs a safe place to hide.

Winter is coming! Ermine sheds his brown summer fur. He grows a thick white winter coat. Ermine's new fur protects him. He blends in with the snow. The tip of his tail stays black. This helps him, too.

It is snowing. Ermine cannot find any mice. A **pika** runs across some rocks. Ermine chases the pika. He follows it through the narrow spaces between rocks. He catches the pika in a hole.

One day, a **wolverine** hunts near Ermine. The wolverine dives for the black tip of Ermine's tail. He thinks it is the body of an animal. He sails over Ermine. He cannot see the rest of Ermine's white body in the snow!

The wolverine tumbles into the snow. Ermine runs away. He hides in a den under the ground. He peeks out from the den. He cannot smell predators. It is safe for him to come out.

Chapter 3

Danger!

Ermine travels over the snowy tundra. It is cold. The snow is deep. Ermine is still hungry for mice. He searches for a home range. This is where he will live and hunt.

One night, Ermine smells some prey. He follows the scent along the ground. It smells like food, but it does not look like an animal. Ermine walks slowly and carefully. He is not sure what he has found.

Ermine catches another scent. It is a new smell. This scent scares him. He runs away. Ermine's sense of smell has saved him. The strange smells came from a trap set by a hunter!

Ermine walks and walks through the snowy tundra. Other ermines chase him away. This is their home! Ermine must find his own home.

Chapter 4

Home at Last

It is March. The air is warmer. The snow starts to melt. Ermine sheds his white fur. His brown summer coat begins to grow. Now he will blend in with rocks and plants on the tundra.

Ermine walks through a field of short grass. He smells wildflowers. Then he smells the scent of mice! He climbs to the top of a large rock. He sees a mouse.

Ermine watches the mouse. He pounces. He lets out a loud shriek. The noise scares the mouse. Ermine is fast. He lands on the mouse with his front feet.

Ermine smells the scent of mice all over the field. He pounces on many mice. Finally, he is full. He saves some of the mice for later.

Ermine makes dens all around the field. Some dens are under the ground. Some dens are in cracks between rocks. He will sleep in the dens. He will also keep his food there. Ermine has finally found a home of his own!

Glossary

Den: a safe place for an animal to sleep and store food.

Ermine: a small, short-tailed weasel.

Pika: a small mammal that looks like a rabbit with short ears.

Shrew: a mammal that looks like a mole.

Tundra: an area of northern America that has short grass, small plants, and many rocks. The tundra is very cold.

Wolverine: a large member of the weasel family that has very dark fur.

Wilderness Facts
About the Ermine

Ermines are members of the weasel family. The ermine is also called the short-tailed weasel. It is one of several weasel species that are found in Alaska and Canada.

Ermines can live in different kinds
of habitats. They live in the rocky,
grassy tundra and the boreal forest.
This story takes place mostly on the
tundra. Ermines are strong animals.
They only weigh about 7 ounces,
but they can run as far as 300 yards
with a large mouse in their mouths.

Ermines have short legs and long, thin bodies. They can slip into dens and burrows. They can hide in narrow spaces between rocks. They can catch small animals, such as voles, in these places. Ermines must eat a few times each day in order to survive. Larger animals, such as wolverines and gray wolves, hunt ermines.

Animals that live near ermines in the tundra region include:

Arctic foxes

Black-tailed deer

Caribou

Dall sheep

Gray wolves

Lynx

Mountain goats

Reindeer

Snowshoe hares

Snowy owls

Voles

White-tailed deer